Legacy

Pat Mullan

Legacy
By Pat Mullan

ASIN: 0983865256
ISBN: 978-0983865254

An *ATHRY HOUSE* book

For ***Ronan Patrick,***
my grandson and fellow writer.

LEGACY

Pat Mullan

Introduction

LEGACY   Pat Mullan

An Introduction to Legacy

Legacy is a full-hearted, generous collection of prose and verse by Pat Mullan, a highly regarded writer of thrillers. It is a moving anthology of brilliant writing in three movements. One might almost say that it is symphonic. The first movement is one of lyrical poems—deeply felt, sad, and personal—expressive of a wistful, lyrical soul. The second movement is a group of powerful prose poems. The third group, "from the archives," is a collection of essay-like pieces from the past but drawn into the present. Combined, they comprise a legacy of profound thought and deep emotion.

Let's engage for a moment with Part One, "a few poems . . ."

"Solitude" brings to mind *The Private Papers of Henry Ryecroft,* George Gissing's withdrawal from new Grub Street. Hear this:

Solitude

I am protective of my solitude now
Savouring it like a well-earned prize
Feeling it would be easy to be a hermit
And shut out all the noise

There are no voices in my ear
None I miss that I hold dear
So let me ask you if I may
Would you seek solitude today?

I've lived in crowded cities
Where tall buildings blocked the light
Where trains screamed through the night
And horns blared down below

So you see why I have fled
Have you fled too?
Or do you still make your bed
Where the bright lights torture you

So let me ask you if I may
Would you seek solitude today?

If you have a proclivity for meditation and are, perhaps, of a certain age, this poem takes you, as Robert Frost wrote, *"back out of all this now too much for us,"* –or out of what we of the present age might call the explosive electronic circus.

Section Two, "prose poems," recalls moments of emotion. This was so, wasn't it? This happened. But these moments have escaped in time, as do our very lives. These moments had a powerful impact on the poet. They are his life. Where are they? They are here in this poetic record.

Pat Mullan makes us feel that we all want such moments back but they cannot be recaptured in full, only in memory. The emotion, the sadness of lost time, is given us as a wistful gift—*à la recherche du temps perdue.* Because of his expressiveness, we all know what the poet knows and feels, and through empathy he gives us back something of our own lives. We appreciate his gift.

Going on to part three, "from the archives," you will find a brief article on the history of the digital revolution in publishing and more personal essays, the most interesting of these being *"Craw: from Childhood Hills,"* a fascinating description of how Mullan came to write the poem, "Craw," which is not included in this anthology; but this reviewer thinks it should have been and presents it here:

Craw

I was born in Craw
on a hill-farm in the heather
of an Ulster mountain

LEGACY   Pat Mullan

The old people said my great-grandfather
had built the first wee house there: a craw,
a thatched-roofed pighouse made of scraws.
And named these hills forever.

But you won't find Craw on any map;
the townland, the postal district
and the parish:
none of them are Craw.

On a clear day you can see *Slieve Snacht,*
the mountain of snow, over there
in Donegal. They say my mother's father
came from there. They called him

Wee Cocky. They said it was because
he was so dapper. But I knew different.
Craw stared across the Foyle in envy
at Donegal, the Free State.

This fine poem speaks for itself.

The other pieces are a bit more practical
as they pertain to writing and the job of
writing itself. Representative of these
pieces, and outstanding among them, is
"James Dickey's Poetry: the Religious
Dimension." As an epistolary friend of
James Dickey's, I can vouch for the
ringing truth presented here.

These pieces should be read and
understood in the way in which, in
general, the last movement of a symphony

sums up or the last part of a mystery explains all.

The great poet, Theodore Roethke, wrote

> "And see and suffer myself
> in another being, at last."

If you read *Legacy* you will see and suffer yourself with this fine poet and essayist.

E.M. Schorb

E. M. Schorb is a poet and novelist. His *Time and Fevers: New and Selected Poems*, was chosen as a 2007 Eric Hoffer Book Award winner. *Murderer's Day* won the Verna Emery Poetry Prize. His poems and prose have appeared in *Best American Fantasy* , as well as *The American Scholar*, *The Beloit Poetry Journal*, *The Chattahoochee Review*, *Chelsea*, *The Literary Review*, *The Massachusetts Review*, *The Southern Review*, *The Sewanee Review*, *The Texas Review*, *The Virginia Quarterly Review*, and *The Yale Review*, among other journals. His honors include Fellowships in Literature from the Provincetown Fine Arts Work Center and the North Carolina Arts Council, and grants from the Ludwig Vogelstein Foundation, the Carnegie Fund for Authors, and Robert Rauschenberg & Change, Inc. (for illustrations in *The Poor Boy)*.

LEGACY Pat Mullan

Legacy

LEGACY   Pat Mullan

Dear Reader,

Giving this collection the title *Legacy* may raise your expectation. A literary legacy is something that an author leaves behind. I have not left. So please consider this as something I leave for your future and my own. Like my previous collection *Knowing*, let me say that this is not a poetry collection.

Yes, there are poems here. And other writing too. To start I have selected a few poems from prior collections and publications. A few that have found favor from many readers.

I believe that we live in parallel universes. I also believe that we are about to colonize other planets, to embark on a future of exciting exploration and new possibilities. I do let this sensibility creep into my writing mind and I'm sure you'll recognize it here.

I don't think that any of my poems need an introduction. My work is simple, accessible, and unencumbered with intellectual reference; you won't need a degree in English literature to enable you to understand it. **Galway Kinnell**, whose *Selected Poems* won the 19 83 Pulitzer Prize for poetry, takes issue with what he regards as two major misconceptions about poetry: first, that it is unread and, second, that in order to be good, poetry should be unreadable: *"After the appearance of the great modernists, Eliot and Pound, when you* *really had to study poetry in graduate school to understand it, the audience for poetry was cut drastically, so when I started writing in the 50's, poetry did have a small, specialized following.   Since then there has been a dramatic change ..."*

I do hope that you find that everything here has a good, hard sense of poetry.

Pat Mullan,
Connemara, Ireland
January, 2019

"...a few poems from prior collections and publications."

LEGACY   Pat Mullan

The Legacy

Every Sunday
You took me on your knee
And read the Beano and Dandy to me

For an hour you were my guide
Reading Desperate Dan to me and
I looked at you with pride

While you took me on a journey
To another world inside

Did you know you were lighting the fire
That burns inside me now.

Awakening

Sometimes our fingers touch
reaching across the morning light
connecting us instinctively
in ways that only our DNA
can best explain
we are supernatural then
able to walk on water
able to soar where our
bodies can not go
and I feel us merge at the dawn
deeper and more knowing
than at any other time
and for a brief moment
I understand life's mystery.

Bicycle Ride

I sat on the cold handlebars
my thighs bone-tight to the metal
as you pushed me

Your breath spluttered
hot on my neck
like the engine in
your old Morris Minor

Up and up that brae
you pushed till you seemed
to stand still on the pedals
almost waiting to fall

Hailstones beat down
on my bare legs
till they were scourged red
but I don't remember the pain

I only remember your strength
and your closeness.
We were never like that again

Socks

"Socks make the man", she said.

"If you have a cow, you'll get a cow", she said.

My mother's markers for life,
She's been gone seven years
And it cuts as sharp as a knife
But she left behind her wisdom
To help wash away the tears

She needed very few words
To convey the way she felt
She taught me how to tie my laces
And how to milk a cow
And how to fight my corner
To stand and never bow

Blackout

I rode the New York subway that night just like every night.

My lifeline from Manhattan to the Bronx; oblivious of its clacks and clonks and its crush of human bodies, I trusted it to take me safely through.   I watched my fellow passengers squeeze tighter together at every station, making room where there was none, hanging on to a space hard won, warily watching each new face that joined us as the doors slammed shut.

I rode the New York subway that night just like every night.

A squeamish stomach in the morning would never serve me well as I pushed into the garlic smell from those who'd eaten an alien meal, and I often guarded against an opportune feel. But in that very same milieu I learned a deeper lesson too, when a young man gave up a hard earned seat to get a lady off her feet, or when I'd observe the unlikely reader, one with hard worked hands, use chipped finger nails to turn the page.

I rode the New York subway that night just like every night.

LEGACY   Pat Mullan

At each new station the doors slid open to let some disembark and many others board and I'd watch the passing parade on the platform, strident, smart, sluggish, anxious, impatient, briefcases or bags, or nothing at all, newspaper clasped or open, or none at all, studiously avoiding each other, the body language of survival.

I rode the New York subway that night just like every night.

Sometimes the train would stop dead between stations without explanation and we'd wait in the stifling heat, silently suffering, sweating together, waiting patiently for a reprieve, always knowing that it would come, trusting that train to see us through before we succumbed to claustrophobia or lost our cool and blew it too; and then, that numbing feeling as we moved on, and the tunnel lights flashed by, hypnotizing us as we thundered through the ink-black tunnel.

I rode the New York subway that night just like every night.

Poems, penny each

LEGACY   Pat Mullan

I hear Ireland calling
with admiration for Walt Whitman

I hear Ireland singing, melodies in the air,
I hear the harp's strings twanging at my heart,
I see fiddlers by the fireside, their faces
Glistening from the open fire, and I hear
the tenor singing the story of his clan,
I see the young girl battering out
her sean-nós steps to the beat.

I hear the swish of the slane out in the bog,
The turf cutter bending low to sever the sod
And the lark rising high in a song of praise
While the west wind beats its way through
The ash and the oak, its thunder drowning
us with its wild Atlantic drum-beat.

I hear Ireland singing of a brand new day,
I see the sheep farmer whistling to his dog,
Rounding up his strays at the end of day
And I hear the young lambs bleat, shouting
0ut like children at play on the city streets

In Maumean, this Valley of the Birds,
gay and glorious song, their joy to be alive,
and I can see the ancestors, the Gaels who
named this valley in their own tongue, yes
I know they're here now, walking beside me,
Listening to the eternal Spring harbinger

I hear the shipyards ring with the harmony
Of the launch   and I see the linen halls
Turn the lint into works of art…and I watch
The Titanic sail to a voyage that was doomed

LEGACY   Pat Mullan

And I wonder: did St. Brendan foresee
These icebergs on his voyage of discovery
Did he feel the dark that lurked beneath
Did he pray for all who sailed

I yearn for the Ireland of Tone where
Protestant, Catholic, and Dissenter
Can live together in harmony where
Old tribal hatreds turn to dust and
We find that we are all the same

And I wonder, are birds singing today over
The Garden of Remembrance, *to the goodly
company of the dead*

The Colour of Ireland is changing

For Kirsten Mate Maher, the 21 year-old African-Irish woman,
who was crowned the 2018 International Rose of Tralee

Caoimhe, the most Irish of names,
 Adorned the badge on her breast
As her finely manicured fingers
Returned my change at checkout
And I absorbed the bronze of her face
And the lips too sensuous to be Irish
And I suddenly realized that

The colour of Ireland is changing

On the narrow streets of Dingle
A young black man struggled
To assemble the buggy
That would soon seat his little
Dark son with the sandy hair
As his blonde Irish mother emerged
From the car to take his hand
And I saw what I already knew

The colour of Ireland is changing

On the same street, minutes later
I stepped aside to let a young Asian
Mother lift her child from the car seat
As his dark haired Irish father
Looked on with parental pride
And I too felt proud to know that

The colour of Ireland is changing

LEGACY   Pat Mullan

In a land once thought to be imprisoned
By the dogmas of the past and
The social hobbles of the narrow lanes
We've seen it break those bonds asunder
And find wider paths to take to a new land
Of diversity and tolerance where

The colour of Ireland is changing

We planted a new milestone in 2016
When we voted for same sex marriage
And again in 2018 when we removed the 8th
And knew we'd climbed to a new high
The first nation to reach this summit
And you could almost see the rainbow
That shadowed our Tricolour flag
And I knew even then that

The colour of Ireland is changing

And now we are led by our Taoiseach,
Leo, a proud Irishman, son of an Indian
Father and an Irish mother, a leader
Who adds a rich lustre to our nation
And throws no shadow from our summit

The colour of Ireland has changed

Listening to the Silence

I hear no bleats from sheep
Nor moos from cows tonight
I hear no songbirds singing
Nor hooves on the road below

I only hear the sound of the silence

I listen to the silence now
And I know that I can hear it
As it wraps me in its blanket
And takes me far away

I only hear the sound of the silence

It whispers stories of the past
And shows me doors into the future
And I know that it protects me
I can hear it tell me so

I only hear the sound of the silence

The clock on the mantle-piece
Ticks the time away
In harmony with the silence
As it strives to fade away

I only hear the sound of the silence

Solitude

I am protective of my solitude now
Savouring it like a well-earned prize
Feeling it would be easy to be a hermit
And shut out all the noise

There are no voices in my ear
None I miss that I hold dear
So let me ask you if I may
Would you seek solitude today?

I've lived in crowded cities
Where tall buildings blocked the light
Where trains screamed through the night
And horns blared down below

So you see why I have fled
Have you fled too?
Or do you still make your bed
Where the bright lights torture you

So let me ask you if I may
Would you seek solitude today?

LEGACY   Pat Mullan

Leaves

Little eddies and
Whirlishes of wind
Scattered the leaves
Here and there

Taking my thoughts along
Urging me to accompany them
And, for a moment, I did
Letting them scatter my words
High into the clouds

Until I'd left myself behind
And joined them in frolic
And abandon, seeking
These verses until I
Heard Aeneas say to me

One thing I ask of you, not to inscribe
Your visions in verse, on the leaves
In case they go frolicking off
In the wind *

*AENEID Book VI by Seamus Heaney

Contemplating my navel

When people speak of mindfulness
As though they'd discovered something new
I think of my navel and wonder

At how it connects me to everything
Yes, I know it started as my umbilical cord
As I jumped out of the womb, tethered
Like an astronaut embarking on a space walk

And I was an astronaut, jumping
From one universe to another, suspended
Between them, until my cord was cut

And I was abandoned on this planet Earth
Severed from my mother ship, left with
That closed port of exit, my navel

Now, when I am mindful
I close my eyes and go on a journey
Through my navel to those other universes

Parallel, these Earth people call them
But I exist in every one of them
My navel is a virtual portal

So when people speak of mindfulness
I contemplate my navel

Idle hands

'Man's brains are going to leave his hands idle'
Quote from my grandfather, Pat Lynch.

As Seamus Heaney said: *I've no spade to follow men like him, Between my finger and my thumb, The squat pen rests, I'll dig with that.'*

I have no squat pen to follow Seamus nor a spade to follow my grandfather and I find my brains too often idle with no field to furrow, no ditch to dig; no words newly forged in the kiln, tempered in the fire of life.

That's when I wish my hands were busy, calloused from a good day's work, sculpting the hedges, mowing the lawn, never idle from dawn to dusk; and my brains never needing to search in that bottomless box of words.

My grandfather was a man of wisdom who could see the road ahead, who would ask *'how could our brains replace our hands, how could our head replace our hands, how would we fill our days with honest work, how could we feel replete, would machines replace our hands'*

Graveyards

The sun shines through the trees
In the village of Eglinton
And I feel a gentle breeze

At the Church of Ireland gate
Where I'd come to find
My great-grandfather's grave

And I hope it's not too late
Will his headstone still stand
Will it mark his resting place

A man of mystery in my past
What do I hope to find
Is this a gesture of respect

To show him I'd crossed the line
In a land of forbidden borders
Where he must have felt unwelcome

Snow

I heard that two feet fell
In Buffalo tonight, and
Eight people died, four
From heart attacks, as
They shovelled

Yet the skies are blue, and
The sun shines through,
Here in Blooming Grove
But snow will fall here too

Should I escape to a place
Where the sun still shines
Through the broken ozone layer
To find revenge in my
Damaged squamous cells

Is it time to go
Where the snow never falls
Where the sun never rises
Where the sun never sets,
Where tidal waves don't drown me
Where no avalanches bury me

LEGACY   Pat Mullan

I will sail to distant lands
With the next Columbus
Where there's neither sun nor snow
Where life is bathed in a healthy glow
And we do not kill for food

And if I find such distant land
And bathe in its healthy glow
Might I suspend my disbelief
And admit that I'm in heaven.

Stones

Why am I compelled
To touch and hold their hard surfaces
To feel their consolation

Dry stone walls
Divide our fields
And mark our ancient roads

Here and there
Artisans of stone
Have sculpted works of art

These stones comfort me
They do not fence me in
Their symmetry protects me

Connemara rocks have exotic names
Such as pillow lavas, tuffs
Greywackes and mudstones.

Granite and quartz compete
For their right of birth and each carries
Deep veins of ancient origin

Connemara marble overshadows
All and has become the chosen stone
From our fireplace to Viscaya

Throughgoin', Forenenst, Thole

It's the language,
            It's the language.

As I stand here in Bellaghy
In Seamus Heaney's HomePlace
I am forced to think about
The way that Seamus used words
To get inside
            our hearts,
                  our minds,
                        our deepest core.

The way he chose works that
            seared our spine and
            sent an alarm to
                  our deepest core.

Words that clashed off each other
            like cymbals
                  and swept us to places
                  not of the ordinary
                        but always of the marvelous

My mind travels back to the
Language of my mother, to the
Words of my great-aunts,
Words now almost extinct

Words forged in Ulster from the
Language of the Irish and the Scots
Words forged from the fires of history

A throughgoin' wee boy,
                'Throogin'
My mother would say
And that one word was all
That we needed to portray
A boy in trouble all day

I search for words these days
To communicate what I mean
But the English language fails
To give me a word that fits
Until I look elsewhere to
The language of my birth.

Listening to the wind

They cancelled Therapeutic Riding today

They feared the ponies would get spooked
by the wind   so now

We're in the Inagh Woods
Walking into the wind and

I see your lips speak to me
With words that are blown away

My body tilted at an angle is
Disabled in some way, allowing

Me to feel empathy for those
Who lost their riding therapy today

The wind speaks to me
Through the trees, imploring me

To listen to the voices
Of those who are dumb

To hold the hands
Of those who are blind

To shelter those who fear
To help those who cannot hear

The wind has eased now
And my body walks erect
But I have learned the lesson
Of listening to the wind.

Broken White Line

A three-year old died today
Killed head-on by a driver
Who passed on a blind corner
At the end of a broken white line

An only child,
    A mother broken,
        A family severed
            A line broken

I hear Dylan in the air
As I cry out loud
Against the dying of this light
That a broken white line could
Be guilty of such a crime

The Taste of the Day

That last mint in bed at night
Takes away the taste of the day
The spices that linger on the tongue
Weren't there when you were young

Five-year Plan

What will your epitaph say
Have you thought about it at all
Or do you consider it presumptuous
To leave a message behind

Are you inspired by epitaphs
That make you wonder about
The mystery of our humanity

Are you left deep in thought
When you visit Seamus Heaney's
HomePlace and read his headstone:

Walk on air, against your better judgement

Or do you want to be the horseman
Who didn't pass by but stopped instead
To visit Yeats's grave and read his words:

Cast a cold eye, on life on death, horseman pass by

So, dear reader, I leave this Legacy to you
and, if you must know, there will be no
headstone after my cremation.
Were there to be, these words would do:

He was working on a five-year plan

The Flat Crust

How I loved the flat crust
Of the bakeryman's bread
And I'd wait every Friday
For his delivery van

The overwhelming smell
Of the fresh loaves inside
Drugged me so well
And I stood there wide-eyed

I watched the bakeryman reach
For his long wooden ladle
And slide it deep inside
To capture my crusty loaf

Slices that were thin
And slices that were fat
Fell on the breadboard
As we sat   each of us
Hoping
          to get the flat crust

And that's why I have learned
To pursue the flat crust of life
To feel its taste in my mouth
And sense its captivating smell

Lost at Breakfast

Oh, how I lose myself

I get trapped by Galway Kinnell
Reading his Oatmeal as I try
To eat my morning oatmeal
And I forget to put the milk away

Oh, how I lose myself

Our poetry reading at breakfast
Is the food that starts our day
Blended with organic oats
It fuels our body and our mind

Oh, how I lose myself

Kinnell said that oatmeal
Should not be eaten alone
That an imaginary companion is best
So he ate with John Keats and said that
He'd invite Patrick Kavanagh to join him
So I have invited Galway Kinnell to share
His Oatmeal with me today

Oh, how I lose myself

Days of Sun and Sadness

In memory of Charles Lynch

How do you say goodbye
For the very last time
Have you thought about that
Or have you buried it deep
In that hard ground of the mind

Then let me tell you about Charlie
And you'll learn how to say goodbye
You'll learn how to stand tall
Your head unbowed, your heart unbroken

Charlie was my cousin, my defender,
My protector at Primary School
But we went our separate ways
When I emigrated to Canada
I said goodbye as he stood tall
An Irish Guard at Windsor Castle

Charlie filled his life with service
From Mayor to Council Chairman
School Governor to Day Care Chairman
But those offices do not define Charlie
He carried them lightly

His real legacy was his work for others
His passion for the plight of the Gurkhas
Led him to lead Friends of the Gurkhas
And raise thousands for their welfare and
His name is now revered in Nepal villages

LEGACY   Pat Mullan

Two years before we lost him
Charlie knew he was departing
He did not hide away, bravely
He went public   not to seek pity
But to stand above it all
And teach us how to say goodbye

A Gurkha played the bagpipes
And his granddaughter played a drum
At the funeral he had organized
A gentle, warm service of remembrance

Two hundred people came to Meade Hall
To celebrate his life, to share memories
And be entertained by a jazz band
Selected by Charlie to play for us

Charlie has taught us how to say goodbye
I don't need to think about that
His life has shown me the way
I will never bury it deep because
There is no hard ground in my mind

LEGACY　　　　　　Pat Mullan

Prose poems

LEGACY

Pat Mullan

The Study Hall at St. Columb's

For all those boarders who suffered at St. Columb's

Imprisoned every evening, desk by desk, side
by side, we sat, nail-biting, silent and the
priest sat, high on the dais like an officer in a
Roman galley, students like oarsmen down
below and I thought that he must see that
boy, four desks away, face bright red, head
dropping down, then waking up again, almost
in rhythm with my imaginary oarsmen and I
struggled with my homework, nobody to ask
questions, silence, no talking permitted no
library, no research, only my textbook, my
paper, my pen, my imagination, my fear until
the Dean strode in, pushing Jesse ahead of
him, John Kelly to him, always Jesse James to
us to make an example out of him to put
fear into us twelve with a leather strap, six
on each hand and I could feel the pain in my
heart's core from the twelve I had gotten, six
on each hand, from the Dean for the crime of
walking across the green, green grass of the
front lawn and I could feel it each time that
strap lashed into Jesse's hands but Jesse
never flinched and the Dean was not satisfied
he wanted humility, pain, tears, fear from
Jesse and then I knew that Jesse had won,
won for all of us

Tribes

They were packed tight in the pub in
Edinburgh that night when I squeezed in at
the bar to get a pint   loud noise and raucous
laughter   filled   the   place   with   banter
bartenders rushed back and forth as orders
stacked up   my hand held high waving a
twenty was ignored   I held it higher and
shouted louder   the man to my right, in a
strong Ulster accent said *louder* and then
followed up with *just out for the weekend ?*
too close to be ignored   I yelled louder and
answered *no, just visiting family*   I'd been
back from the States long enough for the
Ulster in my voice to break out of the
American   finally my pint arrived and I was
about to   force myself away from the bar
when he asked *what lodge do you belong to*
Startled, I knew that he had expected me to be
a member of his tribe   why disappoint him I
answered *ach, I've never been much of a
joiner so I don't belong to any lodge*   and I
moved away, leaving him unrequited.

Birdman

A robin comes to watch me working in the
garden   and she comes again the next day   I
just know she's a lady   she plants herself
nearby   and almost dances in the air as she
circles me   jumping from bush to bush   and
finally settling back again   so I speak to her
and you'd almost believe she listens

She follows me into the greenhouse and flies
around excitedly   won't leave   hides in the
tomato plants   I speak to her, ask how she is,
tell her that she could leave the greenhouse
but she refuses   waits until I leave

And then there was the Manhattan bird that
perched on my left shoulder as I walked
across town, at midday, from Tenth to
Lexington   a small bird that stayed on my
shoulder and looked up at me   I felt as
though I'd been granted some strange power
and people stared at me in disbelief   some
pointed to me and said 'birdman'   and I
smiled back in confidence   but expecting the
little bird to fly away at any moment   but it
did not   it stayed till I reached my office on
Lexington and 53rd Street   only then did it
leave   flying up into a leafy tree that had
been preserved or planted in the atrium of my
office building   but that little bird left me
with the knowledge that all living things on
this planet are more deeply connected than we
know ..

LEGACY   Pat Mullan

Stream of Consciousness

LEGACY   Pat Mullan

Do you wonder

*Do you sit on the hill of Solitude and watch
the world close in   Do you look into the future
and see the light grow dim   Do you reach
across the room and feel the shadows there
Do you stop in a crowded street and see the
people stare*

Do you dream of places far away where days
are long and life is gay   do you look deep
inside and try to find the answer   do you look
outside to ask the question   do you think
sometimes that gravity will fail   do you walk
as though on air and wonder if you are

*Do you sit on the hill of Solitude and watch
the world close in   Do you look into the future
and see the light grow dim   Do you reach
across the room and feel the shadows there
Do you stop in a crowded street and see the
people stare*

Would you climb the highest mountain to
reach the nearest star   would you follow
Scott and Amundsen   would you really go
that far   would you take off on a rocket from
Cape Canaveral   would you sell your soul to
the devil   would you really stoop so low
would you let them stretch you on the rack
would you go to hell and back

LEGACY   Pat Mullan

*Do you sit on the hill of Solitude and watch
the world close in   Do you look into the future
and see the light grow dim   Do you reach
across the room and feel the shadows there
Do you stop in a crowded street and see the
people stare*

Did you rock the cradle with your knees when
you were only one   did you stand against
your brother on the field at Appomattox   did
you fight for Independence inside the Alamo
did you stand upon the gallows with the
Battalion San Patricio

*Do you sit on the hill of Solitude and watch
the world close in   Do you look into the future
and see the light grow dim   Do you reach
across the room and feel the shadows there
Do you stop in a crowded street and see the
people stare*

Do you wonder where you came from   do
you feel that you're alone   do you understand
infinity   do you believe you have a soul   do
you pray to any diety   do you seek a spiritual
space   do you wonder where you came from
do you wonder where you're going   do you
believe there's no tomorrow   do you feel that
this is all there is

*Do you sit on the hill of Solitude and watch
the world close in   Do you look into the future
and see the light grow dim   Do you reach
across the room and feel the shadows there
Do you stop in a crowded street and see the
people stare*

Equilibrium

How do we maintain our equilibrium in this
crazy, crazy world

Is augmented reality the new escape   isn't
AR a harsh sound to the ears   young, addicted
players of Pokemon GO follow their crazy
creatures into rush hour traffic never to return

We're floating now I fear   weightless,
anchor-free, tethered no more   no longer
bound by gravity   free to leave this Earth
and explore new worlds out there

We will design our own reality   DNA will
open the door to our future   we will live on
many planets   many Earths   we will live
where there is no oxygen   we will live
where there is no sun   we will live where
there is no religion   we will not know war
we will live in peace   we will live in John
Lennon's world

Imagine there's no heaven   it's easy if you
try   no hell below us   above us only sky
imagine all the people   livin' for today
imagine there's no countries   it isn't hard to
do   nothing to kill or die for   and no religion
too   imagine all the people livin' life in peace

Does the past exist

Does the past exist, I wonder, or is it a library
of videos, some special, some not so special
organized to entertain or even to frustrate,
filled with laughter or sorrow, or people we
loved, disliked, or even hated. Why would we
store these images and why do they run
without our wish   why do they interrupt when
we don't want them   why can't we retrieve
one that we do want   do you know what I
mean   do you have a library of your past   do
you share a past event   are we connected in
some way   is the past imaginary   did it
really exist

Dream Sequence

I know I'm in Manhattan, but where   I walk
and walk until I find myself in an unknown
neighborhood   is it uptown or downtown   is
it safe or dangerous   suddenly two men walk
beside me, telling me not to step on the
flowers in the middle island   but there are
no flowers   only garbage and rubble in the
middle island   I cross to the street with no
people   only abandoned burnt-out houses
gaping windows   no panes   no frames to
find the same two men following me   this
time riding bicycles   but I only see the face
of one of them: round alien features   ginger
mustache and beard   and green   green eyes
saying *"yeah, I grew up here"* *"yeah, they
don't like us now"* *"yeah, they don't like
green-eyed people"*

,

LEGACY   Pat Mullan

From the Archives

LEGACY   Pat Mullan

The New Publishing Age

In June I flew from Ireland to New York. As usual I stuffed a paperback - a fat one, about 400 pages - into my carry-on bag. I had really wanted to take a hardback I'd been reading at home but that was impractical.

As my fellow travellers and I waited at the boarding gate in Shannon, many of us fumbled with our books, newspapers, boarding passes, and passports. Even those of us with a practiced expertise dropped our bookmarks or momentarily panicked when we thought we'd mislaid our boarding pass.

But, in the midst of all of this, one mature, conservatively dressed lady of middle-age sat unflustered and unencumbered, completely absorbed in the book she was reading: an electronic book, an e-book reader, slim, practical, elegant. I envied her and promised myself that I would join this digital revolution.

I had written previously, on Backspace, about the Amazon Kindle, when I had heralded its arrival. But my promise to join this digital revolution did not mean that I had a sudden impulse to buy a Kindle or a Sony reader and abandon the Agricultural Revolution and Industrial Revolution. The Digital Revolution marked the beginning of the Information Age.' And I would call it the beginning of a New Publishing Age. And this New Publishing Age is accessible to all because it has arrived with its own utility, the internet, the 'information highway', where social networks have transformed this digital revolution into a viral revolution.

Competition to provide the vehicles for that highway, the Kindle, the Sony, the iPad will intensify. Already we see the headlines: 'Amazon sells more Kindle books than hardbacks', 'Publishers negotiating for 'new world order' with Google', iBooks the winner as iPad gains positive feedback', 'iBookstore books cheaper to buy in print and via Kindle, 'W H Smith slashes prices as e-book war intensifies', 'Wylie Agency to bypass publishers and license authors' e-book rights', 'Agents and publishers grapple over 'enhanced' e-book rights', 'Stieg Larsson has continued to dominate e-book sales', 'Simon & Schuster launches digital interactive book', 'Random House digs in over e-book rights', 'US author Seth Godin to bypass 'fundamentally broken

publishers   He states that the present
publishing world is 'fundamentally broken'
and says 'I finally figured out that my
customer wasn't the reader or the book
buyer, it was the publisher. If the editor
didn't buy my book, it didn't get
published'. He continues: 'Authors need
publishers because they need a customer.
Readers have been separated from authors
by many levels - stores, distributors,
media outlets, printers, publishers - there
were lots of layers for many generations,
and the editor with a checkbook made the
process palatable to the writer. Traditional
book publishers use techniques perfected a
hundred years ago to help authors reach
unknown   readers,   using   a   stable
technology (books) and an antique and
expensive distribution system.'

That publishing world is about to change.
Bookseller Borders Group in the US has
unveiled a new concept - a store where
shoppers can mix and burn CDs, explore
their genealogies and even publish their
own novels. Their chief executive George
Jones said, 'If you don't have something
you do better than the other guys, then
frankly the customer doesn't really need
you. This is really intermingling the
typical bricks and mortar with the Internet
and Digital Worlds.' Simon & Schuster

chief executive Carolyn Reidy has appointed Elinor Hirschhorn as chief digital officer. Reidy and Hirschhorn say, "We are determined to avail ourselves to the maximum extent of the digital era opportunities to find, interact, and deliver content instantaneously and around the clock to our readers worldwide. Publishing is at an exciting and transitional moment, with both the nature of books and the relationship among authors, publishers and their readers evolving in new ways"

Open Road Integrated Media, founded by Former HarperCollins chief Jane Friedman to publish e-books drawn from known and unknown authors, is another agent of change that defines my own vision of this new world. Their e-books will be marketed through a proprietary platform "designed to reach consumers where they live, socialize and shop online," Friedman says, "We believe that a story should live everywhere, on all screens, and to that end I look forward to working with authors and agents to create enhanced e-books that place their stories at the front and center of a multi-media universe"   **4th September 2010**

Seamus Heaney has gone home to Derry

Can't believe that Seamus Heaney is gone ...I went to St. Columb's College with him; we were boarders ......he has left us now but, in many ways, he will always be with us ...his words run through my head as I write this ... for the writers out there, he left *Digging* ... but he left his *'mouth wide open'* look at life for all of us.

I wrote this article when Death of a Naturalist appeared. It was published in the USA in The National Hibernian Digest:

Born on a farm in Derry, and educated at St. Columb's College, Seamus Heaney is perhaps the best known of a group of young poets who have formed the vanguard of a new literary revival in Ireland. It seems that violent times and the 'troubles' provide the fertile bed from which literature is born in Ireland. Having been born on a farm in Derry myself and having also attended St. Columb's with Seamus, it is natural for me to maintain a special interest in him.

Out of social revolution against aesthetic and emotional impoverishment, these young poets created Northern Ireland's great magazine, *The Honest Ulsterman*, which came out of Derry in

1968, at the time of French and American student protest and Civil Rights marches in Northern Ireland.

Death of a Naturalist is Seamus Heaney's first published book of poetry. In praise, C.B.Cox of The Sunday Telegraph in Britain has commented: "major poets are as rare as the phoenix, and it is possible that since 1960 only one has emerged in these islands. He is Seamus Heaney, an Irishman who writes with warmth and power about his native landscapes." Indeed, this first book is precisely that: an intense, vivid, descriptive image of his childhood, the terrain and environment of his early youth. The smells, sounds, sights, and sense of being there is conveyed in these poems.

Digging, one of my favourite poems, from this collection, evokes the changing times in Heaney's environment and captures the generation gap and break in the tradition of son following father and grandfather into the same occupation or method of earning a livelihood. *The Barn* illustrates the clarity and strength of image used to animate the descriptive poem and imbue it with an energy and life that invade all the senses.

CRAW: from Childhood Hills

Craw is one of the first poems in *Childhood Hills* and I will talk about 'why it was written' and 'the spark that ignited the vision'. I was born in Derry in the British governed Northern Ireland. Derry lay just north of the border separating those six counties of Northern Ireland from the twenty-six counties that comprised the independent Republic of Ireland, commonly called the 'Free State'. Derry's sister county of Donegal lay in the Republic of Ireland, just on the other side of that border.

One of my earliest memories was the sight of the snow capped mountain called *Slieve Snacht* in the far distance in Donegal. I could see it on those 'daily miles to Craigbrack school'. Donegal to me was in that 'free state', a reminder that I was not free, that I lived in an 'unfree state'. When I was a young boy going to Craigbrack school I knew nothing about that 'free state'. I knew nothing of its history. Irish history was not taught in the schools of the 'unfree state'. But I wondered what it meant to be 'free'. That word captured my imagination. I felt that it must be the same kind of 'free' that I imagined existed in America, the land of the cowboys and *The Yellow Rose of Texas* (that my mother used to sing all the time). It seemed that people from that 'free state' were different from us, that they were very special people. To me, my own grandfather, Johnny McLaughlin, from Donegal was the most special person of them all. He was a 'free man', a special man, a man of that 'free state' that showed me its mountain of snow, its *Slieve Snacht*, on those long 'daily miles to Craigbrack school'.

I remember him well. I remember his quirky sense of humour, his word *breaksif* that he used instead of *breakfast* , his strongest swearword being *'holy sailor!'*, the dapper way he dressed and carried himself, even in his old age. A proud man, a 'free man', a cocky man. When I learned that the locals used to call him *Wee Cocky* when he came up from Donegal, I thought that it suited him so well. I was told that they called him that because he dressed well and took great pride in himself. They were jealous of him, envious of him. But, in my mind's eye, I thought that anyone who came from that 'free state' had to be cocky. To me, every 'free man' had to be a cocky, proud, confident man. And I saw my grandfather in that light.

LEGACY   Pat Mullan

That cocky image of my grandfather
served me well. Nothing: no one, no
teacher, no priest, no policeman, no school
(especially not St. Columb's College)
taught me to be proud and confident. In
fact, with their *leather straps* at St.
Columb's, the Sunday sermons that said
we were living in *sin*, the image of the
RUC police as *jailers* rather than
protectors - all of these things (and more
that I will never speak of) only reinforced
inside me the feeling that I was a prisoner
in an 'unfree state'. I think as you read
Childhood Hills you will see and feel what
I felt.

The first time I felt 'free' was when I
stepped on the North American soil. In
the years that followed, as I fought within
myself to build a sense of confidence, a
sense of cockiness, my grandfather's *Wee
Cocky* image was there to sustain me.
That's the one overriding confident image
that I took from my childhood. It helped
me through University, it gave me the
strength to overcome my own *inferior*
image , it enabled me to achieve high
office in the American corporate world.
Today it gives me the cockiness to dream
of being a writer and to make the dream a
reality by actually becoming a published
author.

LEGACY   Pat Mullan

As I wrote the poem *Craw* I wondered
again about my *Wee Cocky* grandfather.
I'm sure the locals only called him that
out of jealousy, out of envy, out of an
intent to *label* him, to take him *down a
peg or two*. But that other image of him
being a 'free man' from the 'free state'
never left me. So, even if the locals didn't
call him *Wee Cocky* because he came from
the 'free state' I made my poem do that.
So I took a *poetic liberty* and fused those
two images: the one of cockiness, of
confidence and the one of freedom. After
all the years I spent in America, the *'land
of the free'*, that sense of cockiness of my
grandfather, one of the strengths of being
an American, seemed to me to be
something to be very proud of.

Enough said! Too much maybe! Let's
look at those lines in my poem *Craw*
again:

*On a clear day you can see Slieve Snacht,
the mountain of snow, over there in
Donegal. They say my mother's father
came from there. They called him Wee
Cocky. They said it was because he was so
dapper. But I knew different.Craw stared
across the Foyle in envy at Donegal, the
Free State.*

These lines convey that *poetic liberty* that I spoke of above. On the one hand, when I say '*They called him Wee Cocky*' I do it to convey the sense that the locals were jealous, that they wanted to *label* him, to take him *down a peg or two*;   then immediately I say '*But I knew different. Craw stared across the Foyle in envy at Donegal, the Free State*';   here I am using my *poetic liberty* to suggest that I knew differently, that I knew that the real reason they were *labelling* him, the real reason they were calling him *Wee Cocky* was because he was a 'free man' from that 'free state' - and they were envious of that! Now I do know that the people who *labelled* him *Wee Cocky* probably didn't have that motivation.   But that's where a writer can choose to interpret things on another, deeper level.   So, that to me, is what the poem means; and , that to me, is why I am proud to be the grandson of a *Wee Cocky* grandfather!

June, 2000

The Derry Weave

On our tour of Derry's Walls (built in 1619) we were invited to participate in the weaving of a large wall tapestry hanging near the small graveyard that held the graves of the Donegal family of General Bernard Law Montgomery (Monty).

As we weaved the *Derry Weave* we felt the thread that connects Columba (Columcille) from Derry to Iona; we felt the weave tracing its long story through Ireland and Scotland.

Peace reigned in Derry that sunny afternoon as we walked the new Peace Bridge across the river Foyle and ascended Derry's Walls at the Guildhall The years since the signing of The Good Friday Agreement had brought peace to Derry No armed soldiers patrolled the streets and you could feel the changed atmosphere in the air. People seemed more relaxed, smiling, at ease with each other.

The weave comprised several tapestries. The one we worked on about Columba was only one of them.

The latest update on this amazing project

:The Derry Weave was always a project with community at its heart. The St Augustine's community worked so hard during the weeks of the project. The community of 8,000 visitors came from far and wide to take part and weave in their thread. With typical community spirit right from the outset it was the intention that six of the tapestries would be donated to communities across the city:

The Peace Bridge Tapestry gifted to the people of Derry to hang in the Guildhall.

The Long Tower Tapestry gifted to Aras Colmcille to hang in the new Colmcille interpretation centre.

The Promise Chalice Tapestry gifted to St Columb's Cathedral to hang in the Cathedral.

The Ferryquay Gate tapestry gifted to The Apprentice Boys to hang in their new visitor centre.

The First Derry Presbyterian Tapestry gifted to First Derry Presbyterian Church

The Derry Walls Tapestry gifted to The Honourable the Irish Society.

9 November, 2013

Writing and Ireland

There's no way that one can grow up in Ireland without being surrounded by writers. Everybody writes! And, if they don't, they tell stories. The Celtic oral tradition is alive and well. When I was a little boy in our country farmhouse home, people (neighbours, friends, strangers) would come in of an evening, sit around the fire, and tell stories till the 'wee hours' of the morning. Later Irish writers: James Joyce, John McGahern, Brian Moore, Brendan Behan, Oscar Wilde, Sean O'Casey - and today there's so many, starting with my old schoolmate, Seamus Heaney, and others such as Roddy Doyle. Of course my favourite read is the thriller and I love Irish thriller writers such as Jack Higgins and Victor O'Reilly. But I must not leave out my favourite American writers and there are so many of them: Hemingway, Steinbeck, O'Connor, Clancy, James T. Farrell, and many more. I've been scared by Dean Koontz and by Stephen King and Evan Kingsbury (whom you may know better as Robert W. Walker, author of the INSTINCT and the EDGE series) and I've laughed out loud in bed reading Carl Hiaasen. Lately I've been reading my favourite Irish author, Ken Bruen. At College I read the great Russian writers, such as Turgenev and Tolstoy and began a whole new love affair. I suppose every writer that I read has influenced me. I believe that if one wants to (has to) write, one must read, read, read.

I have always had a desire to write. Putting words together seems to be an innate ability. Over the years I exercised that (or maybe I should say, 'exorcised') in my business life by writing business papers and other creative documents - while my scribbled poems ended up in the 'sock drawer'. Some years ago I left a senior position in finance in the US and returned to live in Connemara in the west of Ireland. I had always wanted to write but I had never had the time. Of course, that was a convenient excuse. I was afraid that, if I ever sat down to write, I'd discover that I couldn't. Now that may seem to be a contradiction to you if I always had an innate ability to put words together. Contradiction or not, that's what I felt. So I forced myself to write. I reserved three or four hours each day for writing. The weeks and months passed and one page turned into ten and ten into fifty. Soon I realized that I had written 25,000 words of my first novel and that I

had created a family of characters. The
new world they inhabited took over my
consciousness. I stayed with it. It's a
lonely pursuit and one that demands lots
of fortitude and stamina. So the muse was
always there with me. But I exorcised it
by scribbling poems that conveyed my
feelings or described an event I had
witnessed. Over the years this became a
kind of poetic diary. I never considered
myself a poet. I still don't. When I think of
poets I think of names like Yeats or
Wordsworth or poets of today: Seamus
Heaney, Eamon Grennan, Joan McBreen.
When I think of American poets I think
of Theodore Roethke, Galway Kinnell,
W.S.Merwin, John Ashbery, James
Dickey, and friends: E.M. Schorb, Ted
Deppe & Annie Deppe,   and Dan
Masterson who once told me "*you can
write - no doubt about it - you have a
voice that is your own and that's
important. I want to help your voice
confine itself to the pure statement that
carries the image to the reader.*" I get
most enjoyment from listening to a poet
talk about the written work and the work
in progress: why a poem was written, the
spark that ignited the vision, the snatch of
overheard conversation, the incident that
retrieves a past memory, the choice of
words and imagery, the simple scene
transformed, the need to be a witness.

I'm a morning person so I do try to write every morning, even if it's just scribbled thoughts for my next poem. I do find that I'm more driven when I'm half way into a novel. The story and the characters take over and, if other matters permit, I just lose the sense of time. When that happens, I can write just as readily in the middle of the day or in the evening as I can in the morning. If I go somewhere in the car and I know I will have to kill some time waiting for something or someone, I'll take my briefcase along and use it to jot notes, plot, write, etc. I have three distinct briefcases, one for my poetry, one for my short stories, and one that contains the flotsam and jetsam of my current novel in progress. As you can imagine, they are all overflowing, some more organized than others. But, in a sense, I'm always writing in my head even when I'm gardening or mowing the lawn, and some of my best novel set-pieces come right out of my dreams. I always keep a notebook on my bedside table for those special dream segments that I happen to remember upon waking. In many ways one must be disciplined and set a writing schedule but one shouldn't be deluded into thinking that that will produce the best or most creative output. Less structure and more development of the writerly mind create a consciousness that is pervasive. Then writing in all its manifestation covers the entire day.

In my early days I only wrote using pen and paper. I would type it later into my computer. The word processor was the most efficient way to revise and cut and paste. But there was something distinct about the symbiosis between my hand, the pen, the paper and my mind; something that harnessed my creative mind, something that was missing when I used the computer keyboard. Since then I have adapted somewhat. I can now write directly into my desktop PC. But I still use pen and paper a lot. It serves me well when I'm on the move.

IN MEMORIAM: JAMES DICKEY

LEGACY   Pat Mullan

IN MEMORIAM: JAMES DICKEY

By Pat Mullan

James Dickey, a poet who raised my consciousness at a time when I was not writing any more, a time when I had abandoned it, a time when the muse had departed. Well, James Dickey has now departed. He died on January 19, 1997. I suppose he was best known for his novel Deliverance but he also wrote about 20 volumes of poetry. *James Dickey's Poetry: The Religious Dimension* is my elegy to the man.

ABOUT JAMES DICKEY

In addition to his novel Deliverance James Dickey wrote approximately 20 volumes of poetry. Among his works of poetry were Drowning With Others (1962),

Buckdancer's Choice (1966), which won the National Book Award, The Eye-Beaters (1970), The Zodiac (1976), Scion (1980), Puella (1982), and The Central Motion (1983). In 1972 he wrote the screenplay for the film adaptation of Deliverance and in 1977 he composed a poem, The Strength of Fields, for Jimmy Carter's Presidential Inauguration. Born in a suburb of Atlanta on February 2, 1923, the son of Eugene and Maibelle Swift Dickey, James Dickey grew up with a love of football, canoeing, archery and other high-action, high-risk activities. In 1942, he enlisted in the Army Air Corps and served in World War II. During this time he began to write but it wasn't until the Korean War that he sold his first poem Shark in the Window to The Swanee Review.

James Dickey eventually became poetry consultant to the Library of Congress. In 1968 he became poet in residence and professor of English at the University of South Carolina. He died on January 19, 1997.

JAMES DICKEY'S POETRY:
The Religious Dimension

By Pat Mullan

"But let me say that I have always been against traditional religion because my religion has been so personal to me. I always felt that God and I have a very good understanding, and the more the ritualistic services go on, the more God and I stand by and laugh. I don't believe that the God that created the universe has any interest in the dreadful kind of self-abasement men go through in religious ceremonies." (1).

Those are the words of James Dickey. They sound strong and unequivocal: he totally rejects traditional religion and the established forms of ritual worship associated with it. He is egotistical and presumptuous enough to vilify those who participate in religious ceremonies and to place himself on an equal level with God. Such ego! Such confidence! One would immediately assume that here was a man who had made up his mind and who possessed none of the doubts that most humans do. No search for God seems necessary for Dickey - he has found Him and they have a *"very good understanding"*. (2). James Dickey has been searching for God all his life and it permeates his poetry; he finds Him too, finds Him everywhere and accords God a stature and a mystique that truly identifies with traditional religious beliefs. *"He can start anywhere and find god,"* writes Norman Silverstein, *"not god, with a small g, but the Lord who creates, intercedes, and aids."* (3). Many of Dickey's poems deal with his total preoccupation with all things, especially nature (of which he writes much); through nature he reflects God's work of creation. According to Arthur Gregor, *"Dickey deals with the magic that results when the observer sees the supernatural expressed in nature, nature, and experiences - is ultimately involved in - this transformation." (4) Dickey's view of God and creation is not a simple, untroubled one, but rather, a vision of loftiness, supernatural themes and of man's unity with the universe. In his poem "Inside the River" (5) he starts off with someone gently edging one foot and then the other into a river, seemingly to bathe or wade. Before the poem ends though, the person has entered the river, evoking a sense of total immersion, almost the biblical form of baptism. The river is a symbol of immortality as these lines show:*

Put on the river
Like a fleeing coat,

A garment of motion,

Tremendous, immortal.

and the dead are also immortal as in :

Live like the dead

In their flying feeling.

and again, towards the end of the poem,
when birth and death are united by the
grasp of a root:

Weight more changed

Than that of one
Now being born,
Let go the root.
Move with the world

As the deep dead move,

Opposed to nothing.

Dickey's identity with traditional religious
reference points marks the strong presence
of God and creation expressed through his
poem, "In the Mountain Tent" (6), which
describes the poet's innermost mingling
with nature whilst lying inside a tent
during a heavy rainstorm. Here he
describes the shining of water *"like dark,*
like light, out of Heaven" and uses images
such as *"the sustained intake of all breath*

before the first word of the Bible" and *"the tent taking shape on my body like ill-fitting, Heavenly clothes. "* The ending lines of the poem have a Christ-like image of resurrection as he says: From holes in the ground comes my voice In the God-silenced tongue of the beasts. *"I shall rise from the dead, "* I am saying.

Dickey describes this poem as one in which the man in the tent, while lying there, begins the dream of his own death. Being a product of western culture, the man is influenced by Christian doctrines and the belief in the Resurrection. And he, therefore, feels kinship with the animals on the mountainside and a fundamental difference in that he realizes he may rise from the dead and they'll only die. (7) In the words of Peter Davison, "Dickey's work is a search, in a sense, for heaven on earth," (8) Dickey never crosses the supernatural boundary to lend imagery in his poetry to that heaven in the afterlife. When he does deal with such a heaven, he reserves it for the animals in "The Heaven of Animals". (9) It is not the conceptual human heaven of harps and white robes but is expressed as a continuance of the animals' lives in their natural environment. Dickey can best perceive or imagine what would be an ideal animal heaven - simply the continuity of their earthly existence :

Here they are.

The soft eyes open.

If they have lived in a wood
It is a wood.

If they have lived on plains
It is grass rolling
Under their feet forever.

Dickey does not seem to be able to perceive or imagine what would be an ideal human heaven, so he does not deal with it. This is another example of his unresolved conflict with the traditional religious concepts of his childhood. *"The Dantean comic end, a heaven for people, does not enter into Dickey's poetry. It might be that it carries for him (out of a*

Southern Bible Belt culture) connotations of spiritual fixedness," (10) writes Robert W. Hill.

Despite the innumerable Biblical references in his poetry, Dickey disclaims any religious identification: *"I love the Bible, though. But the Bible to me is a great work of literature only."* (11)

He is, however, imbued with religion (his own brand as he defines it):

But the religious sense, which seems to me very strong in my work in some weird kind of way, is a very personal kind of stick-and-stone religion. I would have made a great Bushman or an aborigine who believes that spirits inhabit all things. (12)

This personal religion of Dickey's is Christian, paganistic, Hindu-like, and primitive: a cauldron of supernatural potions that creates in the poet his need to blend man and beast, natural and supernatural, reality and fantasy, into a recipe that leaves him with a fear of death (not physical death, but mortality), a search for a reincarnate continuity of existence and a need to define the state of afterlife. He separates the world created by man from that which exists naturally, yet he will not fully commit himself to either confirming or denying that it is God's world: *I'm much more interested in a man's relationship to the God-made world, or the universe-made world than to the man-made world. The natural world seems infinitely more important to me than the man-made world.* (13)

The theme of resurrection from the dead and of continuity of existence through reincarnation is a magnetic attraction for Dickey. He deals with a very traditional Christian concept of resurrection in his poem, *"Sleeping Out at Easter"* (14) from the collection *Into the Stone*. According to Dickey, the poem describes a father waking up after having slept outside all night at Eastertime. When Dickey was in the advertising business, he slept out, in the springtime, in a sleeping bag in a little pine grove behind his suburban house in Atlanta. In relating that experience, which provided the idea for the poem, Dickey says:

But I didn't wake up feeling that I was Christ. That's something I made up. Still, reading the poem again, I feel that I should have awakened on Easter thinking I was Christ, in the same sense that every man is Christ and Christ is every man, if you're a believer. (15)

Just as James Dickey cannot (and does not wish to) separate himself from his Southern background and identity, neither can he separate himself from his traditional Southern religious roots and early beliefs, as he pronounces that he has:

Church always seemed to me to be very much beside the point. Religion to me involves myself and the universe, and it does not admit of any kind of intermediary, such as Jesus or the Bible. (16)

The pronounced rejection of Jesus is strongly contested by the poetic incorporation of Christ in poems like *"Sleeping Out at Easter"* and *"Walking on Water"*, (17) another poem from the collection, Into the Stone. This poem is literally a narrative about a boy crossing a river by poling while standing on a plank. However, the plank is barely submerged beneath the water and the poem becomes a reflection of the supernatural Biblical ability of Christ to walk on water:

Later, it came to be said
That I was seen walking on water,

Not moving my legs
Except for the wrong step of sliding: \

A child who leaned on a staff,

A curious pilgrim hiking
Between two open blue worlds
\

Even Dickey acknowledges the theme when he describes it: *Later, it came to be said, that I was seen walking on water, Not moving my legs. Except for the wrong step of sliding: A child who leaned on a staff, A curious pilgrim hiking Between two open blue worlds*

"I thought, 'Well, let's take this seriously as a miracle.' It's a kind of natural miracle. He would seem to be like a Junior Christ." (18)

This theme (of Christ walking on water) is also contained in the poem "The Lifeguard" (19) from the collection *Drowning with Others*.

George Lensing writes, *"The lifeguard, in the actions of his own consciousness, suggests the image of Christ, who also walked on waters, and was able to resurrect the dead."* (20)

This poem primarily concerns man's inability to undo things already done, especially to return to life those who have died, a concern that fills Dickey's consciousness and makes him continually aware of how seemingly unfair life can be: relationships with others, the essence of life, are but a fleeting thing owing to the mortality of all things. In *"The Lifeguard"* , Dickey describes the failure of a lifeguard to rescue a child and the guilt that overcomes him because he had also fractured the unquestioning faith of the village children who believed that he could prevent them from harm. So he hides among the boats, waiting till night-time and hallucinating that he could walk out on the moonlight on the river and rescue the child who'd been lost:

I set my broad sole upon silver,
On the skin of the sky, on the moonlight,
\

Stepping outward from earth onto water

In quest of the miracle

This village of children believed

That I could perform as I dived

For one who had sunk from my sight.

Much of Dickey's poetry emanates from personal experience and remembrance. He once participated in diving to try to recover the body of someone who had drowned. The stony feeling in his fingers is recaptured in these lines: (21)

And my fingertips turned into stone

From clutching immovable blackness.

Dickey, himself, commented on *"The Lifeguard"* thus:

"In the delirium of grief ---- he comes to believe ---- that he'll be able to walk out into the water, much as Christ did, and raise the child back to life." (22)

Identifying poetic characters with Christ was always a Dickey tendency. Even in his earliest writings, he once published a long poem in Poetry magazine called *"The First Morning of Cancer"*. In Dickey's words, it was a supposedly visionary poem about a man suffering from a brain tumor and how the affliction affected his mental processes and caused him to think and see different things. Dickey eventually had the man identify himself with Christ. (23)

Richard Howard, in writing about James Dickey, has stated that:

The poet confronts and laments (exults over) the outrage of individual death, of a linear movement within time - each event and each moment being unique, therefore lost. (24)

Dickey's strong association with animal life and nature has provided the poet with a methodology for taking the poetic license of denying the reality of man's mortality and defeating *"the outrage of individual death"*. (25)

Again, Dickey must search for a religious concept to work with, reincarnation, and he said: *Reincarnation is one religious idea I have always loved believing in. I don't know whether the soul passes from one kind of creature to another; I hope it does. (26)*

Dickey deals with this subject in the poem, *"Reincarnation (I)"* from the *Buckdancer's Choice* collection and, again, in *"Reincarnation (II)"* from the collection in *Falling*. In neither of these poems is the man reincarnated again as a human and that shouldn't surprise, given the predominance of animal life as subject matter for much of Dickey's poetry.

George Lensing, in reflecting on this aspect, has written:

In all these poems Dickey suggests that the spiritual affinity between man and animals is sacred and that animal life, in its natural beauty and instinctive wisdom, is one to which humans may aspire and in which they may find their own heightened identity. (27)

"*Reincarnation (I)*" (28) is a somber, thought-provoking poem about a man being reincarnated as a rattlesnake. The narrative focuses on the natural order of life from the vantage point of the snake and, subtly, looks backward to one man's way of life. The snake exists as the poem begins and the only overt reference to a previous life appears in the first stanza:

Still, passed through the spokes of an old
wheel, on and around
The hub's furry rust in the weeds and
shadows of the riverbank,
This one is feeling his life as a man move
slowly away. Fallen from that estate, he
has gone down on his knees
And beyond, disappearing into the egg
buried under the sand

The mission of the snake becomes clear as the narrative proceeds: to lie and wait in the shadow of the old wagon wheel, poised with poisonous intent, to strike the first man to appear:

But mainly, now, from waiting - all the
time a symbol of evil –
Not for food, but for the first man to walk
by the gentle river:
Minute by minute the head becomes more
poisonous and poised.

In his own words, Dickey sees the rattlesnake as a symbol of justice and, in what can only be a definite Biblical reference to the Garden Eden, states: *"The justice of the Lord, in its most striking case, depended on the intervention of the snake."* (29)

It appears that Dickey has interwoven into this poem a cyclical process of life and death, with the snake not only being the instrument of life's continuity through reincarnation but also being the instrument of death through its poisonous fangs. In some way, Dickey also wants this poem to incorporate the justice of the Lord and the mystery of God's world as seen through the drama in the Garden of Eden, which was a place of creation, death and rebirth in a new environment.

"Reincarnation (II)" (30) (30) is about an office worker who is reincarnated as a migratory sea bird. In this poem, the man realizes that he has now become a bird which is a departure from *"Reincarnation (I)"*, where the snake didn't know that he had once been a man.

In speaking about this poem, James Dickey has said: *I tried to show two things in the poem: first, the recognition of this being that he's now a bird and no longer a man, and his realization that he can navigate by means of the stars; second, the gradual fading of his identity as a human being through this long voyage. (31)*

During the bird's long voyage, he navigates by the stars, dreaming at one point that he sees the Southern Cross. Dickey takes advantage of this by having the bird reflect back to his life as a man, wherein he had believed in another Cross, which he now (as a bird) labels false. This can only be another way of Dickey reflecting his ambivalence about Christianity:

He sees the Southern Cross
Painfully over the horizon drawing itself

Together inching
Higher each night of the world thorn

Points tilted he watches not to be taken in

By the False Cross as in
Another life not taken

The theme of reincarnation is one of the ways in which Dickey creates life beyond death. He must create such life because of his fear of total extinction and his inability to conceptualize heaven.

The poet and critic, Richard Howard, describes this fear he finds in *Buckdancer's Choice : Obsession, madness, excess: the burden of Buckdancer's choice is altogether new in the poet, and crowned or ballasted, by a pervasive terror of extinction.* (32)

That *"terror of extinction"* (33) is treated well in the poem *"The Escape"* (34) from the *Buckdancer's Choice* collection. Here, Dickey speaks of the long tradition of burial in the family plot at Fairmont and then of the spontaneous (almost dreaded) secret purchase of his own grave plot at a little country graveyard in Alabama, which he had walked through on a hunting trip:

I walked through the evergreen gates of
the forest ranger's station,
And out to my car, and drove
To the county seat, and bought

My own secret grave plot there

For thirty-seven dollars and a half

And yet he somehow hopes not to die and shows his fear of it in the ending lines of the poem:

LEGACY   Pat Mullan

I remember that, and sleep
Easier, seeing the animal head
Nuzzling the fragment of Scripture,

Browsing, before the first blotting rain

On the fragile book
Of the new dead, on words I take care,

Even in sleep, not to read,
Hoping for Genesis.

Dickey is not being fully truthful when he states that *"the Bible to me is a great work of literature only"* (35). In his long poem *"May Day Sermon to the Women of Gilmer County, Georgia, by a Woman Preacher leaving the Baptist Church"* (36), he returns again to religion and the bible as the fabric underlying the theme of the poem.

Dickey is not making a statement about the literate quality of the Bible but, rather, its religious content and about how people can use the word of God for evil and malevolent ends.

Dickey , himself, has described *"May Day Sermon"* :

. *"May Day Sermon" is about the malevolent power God has under certain circumstances; that is, when He is controlled and "interpreted" by people of malevolent tendencies. In this case God is neither more nor less than a combination of the Old Testament and a half-mad Georgia hill farmer. (37) "Above all, the poem is an indictment of containers, restrictions, barriers including organized religion.*

The father is like the vindictive God of the Old Testament" (38), writes Thomas O. Sloan. In *"May Day Sermon" ,*

Dickey deals with God and the devil against the backdrop of a sermon warning the girls of Gilmer County, Georgia to be wary of affairs with their lovers and relating how a girl gets beaten by her father (whom she subsequently murders) for just such an affair with her motorcycle lover. The strong images of the beating can be seen in these lines:

*On the red clay floor of Hell she
screaming her father screaming Scripture
CHAPter and verse beating it into her
with a weeping Willow branch the animals
stomping she prancing and climbing*

And these lines describe her love affair as
being the work of the devil:

*Die out as her freckled flesh as flesh and
the Devil twist and turn Her body to love
cram her mouth with defiance give her
words To battle with the Bible's in the air:
she shrieks Sweet Jesus and God I'm glad
O my God - darling O lover O angel-stud
dear heart*

Dickey has also stated: *"I wanted to make
the Bible, or a certain interpretation of the
Bible which permits cruelty, the final
focus of the poem."* (39)

When this poem was first published, its
harsh religious overtones raised many
protests, as evidenced by these words of
Thomas O. Sloan:

*Soon after the poem first appeared in the
Atlantic in April, 1967, a man who signed*

himself "the founder of the Poetry Society of New Hampshire" wrote a letter to the editor insisting that the Atlantic apologize to the "good people of the Baptist denomination as well as to the high art of poetry." (40)

There is, therefore, overwhelming evidence throughout James Dickey's poetry supporting the fact that he is engrossed in an attempt to, on the one hand, substantiate his early Southern Christian upbringing and, on the other hand, exorcise himself from it. He has been unsuccessful in achieving neither and his confident statements to the contrary are unfounded. Perhaps these assertions and statements, to use Dickey's own words, are part of the process of inventing conditions under which he can live with himself.

In fact, James Dickey should have the final say in the matter himself:

All poetry, I suspect, is nothing more or less than an attempt to discover or invent conditions under which one can live with oneself. I have been called a mystic, a vitalist, a pantheist, an antirationalist, and a good many other things. I have not been conscious of the applicability of any of these labels, although they very well may all apply. At any rate, what I have always striven for is to find some way to incarnate my best moments - those which, in memory, are most persistent and obsessive. (41)

(1). James Dickey, Self-Interviews , (New York, 1970) , p. 78. (2). Ibid.

(3). Norman Silverstein, "James Dickey's Muscular Eschatology", Contemporary Poetry in America , (New York, 1974), p. 306

(4) Arthur Gregor, "James Dickey, American Romantic," James

(6) James Dickey, Poems 1957-1967

(7) James Dickey, Self-Interviews

(8) Peter Davison, "The Great Grassy World from Both Sides," James Dickey: The Expansive Imagination (Florida, 1973), p. 46 (New York, 1974), p. 109 (New York, 1970), p. 120

(10) Robert W. Hill, "James Dickey: Comic Poet," James Dickey: The Expansive Imagination (Florida, 1973), p. 148

(11) James Dickey, Self-Interviews (New York, 1970), p. 78

(12) Ibid., p. 79

(13) Ibid., p. 67 (14) James Dickey, Poems 1957-1967 (New York, 1974), p. 17

(16) Ibid., p. 78

(17) James Dickey, Poems 1957-1967

(18) James Dickey, Self-Interviews

(19) James Dickey, Poems 1957-1967 (New York,1974), p. 39 (New York, 1970), p. 97, New York, 1974), p. 51

(20) George Lensing, "James Dickey and the Movements of Imagination", James Dickey: The Expansive Imagination (Florida, 1973), p. 168

(22) Ibid., p. 103

(23) Ibid., p. 47

(24) Richard Howard, Alone with America (New York, 1969), p. 91

(25) Ibid., p. 91

(27) George Lensing, "James Dickey and the Movements of Imagination", James

Dickey: The Expansive Imagination, (Florida, 1973), p. 164

(29) James Dickey, Self-Interviews, (New York, 1970), p. 141

(31) James Dickey, Self-Interviews, (New York, 1970), p. 164

(32) Richard Howard, Alone with America, (New York, 1969), p. 91

(33) Ibid., p. 91

(34) James Dickey, Poems 1957-1967,

(35) James Dickey, Self-Interviews, (New York, 1974), p. 203 (New York, 1970), p. 78

(37) James Dickey, Self-Interviews, (New York, 1970), p. 183

(38) Thomas O. Sloan, "The Open Poem is a Now Poem: Dickey's

(39) James Dickey, Self-Interviews, (New York, 1970), p. 184

(40) Thomas O. Sloan, "The Open Poem is a Now Poem: Dickey's May Day

(41) James Dickey, Babel to Byzantium, (New York, 1968), p. 292

BIBLIOGRAPHY

Davison, Peter. "The Great Grassy World from Both Sides", James Dickey:

The Expansive Imagination, edited by Richard J. Calhoun, Florida, 1973.

Dickey, James. Babel to Byzantium. New York, 1968 \

Dickey, James. Poems 1957-1967. New York, 1974

Dickey, James Self-Interviews. New York, 1970

Gregor, Arthur. "James Dickey, American Romantic",

Hill, Robert W. "James Dickey: Comic Poet",

James Dickey: The Expansive Imagination, edited by Richard J. Calhoun, Florida, 1973

Howard, Richard. Alone with America. New York, 1969

Lensing, George. "James Dickey and the Movements of Imagination",

James Dickey: The Expansive Imagination, edited by Richard J. Calhoun, Florida, 1973.

Silverstein, Norman. "James Dickey's Muscular Eschatology", Contemporary Poetry in America, edited by Robert Boyers, New York, 1974.

Sloan, Thomas O. "The Open Poem is a Now Poem: Dickey's May Day Sermon", James Dickey: The Expansive Imagination, edited by Richard J. Calhoun, Florida, 1973.

LEGACY   Pat Mullan

.

LEGACY

Pat Mullan

Pat Mullan

Pat Mullan is a thriller writer, poet, and artist. He was born in Ireland and has lived in England, Canada and the USA. He now lives in Connemara, in the west of Ireland.

You can visit him at:
www.patmullan.com

LEGACY   Pat Mullan

www.ingramcontent.com/pod-product-compliance
Lightning Source LLC
Chambersburg PA
CBHW030635130626
46552CB00002B/856